ORPHAN TRAIN CHILDREN

WILL'S CHOICE

Joan Lowery Nixon

D0017735

A YEARLING BOOK

Painted (handwriting)

In gratitude to Beverly Horowitz,
who shares the dream

Published by
Bantam Doubleday Dell Books for Young Readers
a division of
Random House, Inc.
1540 Broadway
New York, New York 10036

Visit us on the Web! www.randomhouse.com

Educators and librarians, for a variety of teaching tools, visit us at www.randomhouse.com/teachers

---

ISBN: 0-440-41309-5

Reprinted by arrangement with Delacorte Press

Printed in the United States of America

October 1999

10 9 8 7 6 5 4 3 2 1

CWO

A Note from the Author

In the 1850s there were many homeless children in New York City. The Children's Aid Society, which was founded by Charles Loring Brace, tried to help these children by giving them new homes. They were sent west and placed with families who lived on farms and in small towns throughout the United States. From 1854 to 1929, groups of homeless children traveled on trains that were soon nicknamed orphan trains. The children were called orphan train riders.

The characters in these stories are fictional, but their problems and joys, their worries and fears, and their desire to love and be loved were experienced by the real orphan train riders of many years ago.

Joan Lowery Nixon

More orphan train stories by
Joan Lowery Nixon

The ORPHAN TRAIN Adventures

ORPHAN TRAIN CHILDREN

Homes Wanted
For Children

A Company of Orphan Children

of different ages in charge of an agent will arrive at your town on date herein mentioned. The object of the coming of these children is to find homes in your midst, especially among farmers, where they may enjoy a happy and wholesome family life, where kind care, good example and moral training will fit them for a life of self-support and usefulness. They come under the auspices of the New York Children's Aid Society. They have been tested and found to be well-meaning boys and girls anxious for homes.

The conditions are that these children shall be properly clothed, treated as members of the family, given proper school advantages and remain in the family until they are eighteen years of age. At the expiration of the time specified it is hoped that arrangements can be made whereby they may be able to remain in the family indefinitely. The Society retains the right to remove a child at any time for just cause, and agrees to remove any found unsatisfactory after being notified.

Remember the time and place. All are invited. Come out and hear the address. Applications may be made to any one of the following well known citizens, who have agreed to act as local committee to aid the agent in securing homes.

A. J. Hammond, H. W. Parker, Geo. Baxter, J. F. Damon, J. P. Humes,
H. N. Welch, J. A. Armstrong, F. L. Durgin.

This distribution of Children is by Consent of the State Board of Control, and will take place at the

G. A. R. Hall, Winnebago, Minn.
Friday, Jan. 11th, '07, at 10.30 a. m. @ 2 p. m.

H. D. Clarke, State Agent,
Dodge Center, Minn.

Office: 105 East 22nd St.,
New York City.

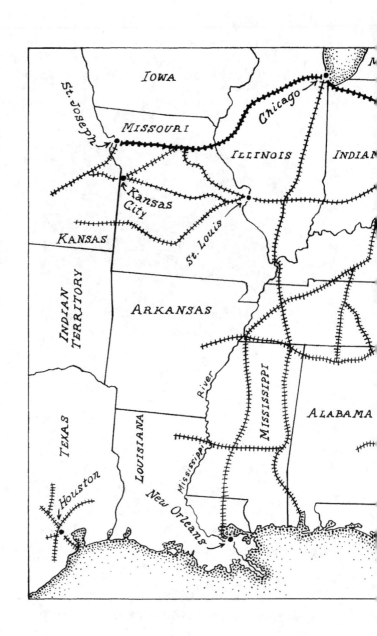

Orphan Train Routes CIRCA 1866

From the Journal of
FRANCES MARY KELLY, JULY 1866

Our train ride to Missouri is long and tiring for the children, but, on the whole, they are taking it in good spirits. At the moment some of the older boys are restless, using their extra energy to tease one another. It is harmless teasing, and they are having fun, so I pretend I do not hear them.

Will Scott is smiling, and that makes me happy. This is the first time I have seen Will smile.

Will is tall for twelve, but much too thin. I think a few good meals will take care of that problem. I was told that Will has recently recovered from a broken leg. He still limps, but otherwise seems to be a healthy boy.

At the Children's Aid Society offices Miss Hunter took me aside. She said, "Will is very sad. He can't believe his father would send him away."

I knew exactly what Will was feeling. I well remember when Ma gave my brothers and sisters and me to the Society to send west to foster homes.

Earlier this evening I saw tears running down

Will's cheeks. I squeezed into the seat beside him and handed him a clean handkerchief. "My brothers and sisters and I shed many tears when we came west on an orphan train," I told him.

"I'm not an orphan," Will said. "I have a father. He works for Carnaby's Traveling Tent Show. Maybe the show will come to my new home and he'll want me to go with him."

I smiled and patted Will's shoulder. "We had a mother who'd wanted us to have a better life than we'd find on the streets of New York. And one day she did come west to join us."

Will looked up hopefully. "Your mother came for you? Then I'll keep looking for my father. Someday he'll come for me, too."

What could I tell Will that wouldn't dim the hope and trust shining in his eyes?

All I could do was give him a friendly pat on the arm and smile. Oh, Will, I thought, I hope and pray that you will soon find a happy and loving home.

CHAPTER ONE

Will Scott stared straight up at the trapeze. It was up so high, just looking at it made him dizzy. For a moment he felt sick.

"Trapeze artists are all the rage in Europe," said Jesse Scott, Will's father. "Mr. Carnaby's going to add trapeze acts to his circus. Think what a great opportunity this could be for you."

Will had seen posters of trapeze artists swinging high in the air. "I don't know how," he blurted out.

"I know you don't," Jesse said. "But you can learn, can't you?"

Will groaned. Jesse kept trying to teach him circus tricks, and Will failed at all of them.

Two years ago Jesse had told him, "We'll start you out as a stand-up bareback rider, Willie." Leading him into a sawdust-filled ring, Jesse had helped Will climb onto the back of the gentlest horse. Then he'd tied a rope around Will's waist and secured it to a long wooden pole.

"Stand up, Willie," Jesse had ordered.

"I can't. I'll fall off." Will had gripped the horse's mane with trembling fingers and stared at the ground far below. He hadn't realized how big the horses were.

"You won't fall," Jesse had said. "You can't fall. You're tied to the mechanic—that pole I just fastened you to. It will keep you from falling to the ground as the horse trots around the ring. Now stand up. Give it a try."

Will's eagerness to please his father had been stronger than his fear of falling from the horse. Slowly and carefully he had managed to stand.

Jesse had planted Will's feet just ahead of the horse's rump. Then he had made a clicking sound. Suddenly the horse had begun to move.

"Keep your feet steady!" Jesse had cried. "Lean toward the center of the ring! Balance! Balance!"

But no matter how hard Will had tried, over and over again he'd lost his balance. In a panic, he would feel the horse's broad back slip out from under him, and he'd sail into the air. The rope would jerk hard around his waist, cutting into his stomach. Hanging nearly upside down, Will had coughed and retched and finally vomited.

In disgust Jesse had lowered the rope, and Will had plopped to the ground. He'd wiped his mouth on his sleeve and curled up into a miserable ball.

"It's no use. You'll never manage it," Jesse had said.

Will's face had burned with shame. Why couldn't he learn that simple trick? He was Jesse's son, wasn't he?

Jesse Scott was the star of Carnaby's Circus. He could ride two horses at the same time, standing with one foot on each saddle. He could somersault from one horse to the other. He could even stand on his head in the saddle while firing a pistol at a target. *Why couldn't I learn to do the same,* Will wondered, *instead of failing my father every time?*

Jesse hadn't given up. He'd tried turning Will into a clown. Clowns were popular in the circuses of France and England, he'd told Will. Jesse had given Will a silly costume to wear, but Will couldn't seem to get the feel of what clowns were supposed to do. No one had thought he was funny.

Then there was Gorgo, the dancing bear. Antonio was Gorgo's trainer. Antonio had shown Will how to get Gorgo to stand on his hind legs and dance. "Try it," Antonio had said, and handed Will a short, black whip. "When you want him to go up, hold the whip high. Down, bring the whip down. Gorgo will follow the whip."

When Gorgo had opened his mouth, Will could see his sharp teeth. He'd been glad that Gorgo was fastened to a sturdy chain. So frightened he could hardly speak, Will cracked the whip once and held it high. Gorgo rose on his back legs, towering over Will.

The sight had so alarmed Will, his hands shook.

He dropped the whip and, to his horror, Gorgo lumbered toward him.

"Back up! Go away!" Will had shouted. His legs had caught on Gorgo's chain, and Will had fallen on his back. He squeezed his eyes shut as the chain pulled Gorgo toward him.

Will's right arm had swelled up and hurt for more than two weeks.

Jesse's impatient voice broke into Will's memories. "Stop daydreaming, Willie! Listen to me. Pay attention."

"I'm sorry," Will whispered.

Jesse sighed. "Climb this rope ladder to the platform over your head. Mario will swing the trapeze toward you. When it's close enough, reach out and grab it. Then push off and swing across to Mario's platform. Understand?"

"What if . . ." Will's voice cracked. "What if I fall?"

Jesse frowned. "Don't even think about falling. But if by some chance you do, you'll land in the net. Now stop wasting time. Go!"

Scarcely breathing and weak with fear, Will

climbed to the platform. He could see the trapeze bar swinging toward him. He tried to reach out and grip the bar the way he was supposed to. But it slipped from his fingers, and he fell. Even his fall was wrong. Instead of landing in the net, he bounced off its tight edge and hit the hard ground below.

Floating in and out of pain, Will said over and over, "I'm sorry, Jesse. I'm sorry."

From a distance Will thought he heard his father say, "Poor Willie. You just can't do anything right, can you?"

CHAPTER TWO

Will leaned forward and watched his father hop, jump, and dance his way up the steps of Mrs. Clutterham's porch.

"Ta-da! Great news, Willie!" Jesse shouted. His black curls bounced and his blue eyes sparkled.

Will couldn't help smiling at the sight of his handsome father. Jesse lived for fun and laughter. He used to make Will's mother laugh until there were tears in her eyes. "When are you going to grow up, Jesse Scott?" she'd say. "You act as if you're only a boy."

His father really wasn't that far from his boyhood. Will often heard people tell Jesse, "You look

9

much too young to be a father to this strapping lad!"

"I married young," Jesse would answer. "Ruth and I weren't much more than babes before we had a child ourselves." He'd sigh and add, "Ah, but Ruth was a lovely girl. We had some grand times together." He'd dance a twirling tap step and people would laugh.

But Will remembered the terrible pain that had been in his father's eyes after Ruth, Will's mother, died. Will remembered waking night after night to hear Jesse crying.

For an instant Will was a four-year-old again, screaming in terror as his mother lay in the street. She'd been hit by a runaway carriage. Blood had gushed from her leg, and no one had known how to stop the bleeding and save her life.

Suddenly Will wanted to ask his father, "Where have you been? Why didn't you ever come to visit me while my leg was healing?" But Jesse looked so excited and happy that Will couldn't bear to spoil his fun. Even though Will was twelve, sometimes he felt as if *he* were the father and Jesse the son.

Patiently Will patted the bench and said, "Sit down, Father. Tell me your news."

"How many times do I have to remind you? Call me Jesse, not Father," Jesse said good-naturedly. "*Father* makes me feel old." He hopped over Will's right leg, which was propped on a small footstool. Then he stopped, looking puzzled.

He's forgotten all about the trapeze accident, Will thought. He fought back the disappointment he'd come to know so well.

An embarrassed flush spread over Jesse's face. He sat next to Will and asked, "How's the leg?"

"Fine," Will answered. "The doctor told me I'll be able to walk without crutches in another week. Fa— Jesse, I'm sorry I was so clumsy." He took a deep breath. "I'll try again with the trapeze, if you want me to."

Will desperately wished he could fit into his father's circus life. Carnaby's Circus was a small outfit that performed in a large, barnlike building on New York City's Lower East Side. Jesse was the ringmaster, did trick riding, and trained the horses. Carlos Carnaby had been able to find acrobats,

11

clowns, two mangy lions, and a trained bear. There were shows every day. The crowds weren't large, but they were steady.

Will was puzzled when Jesse acted as though he hadn't heard his offer. "Has Mrs. Clutterham been taking good care of you?" Jesse asked.

"She's kind," Will said. "And she's a good cook."

Jesse lowered his voice and winked. "Maybe so, but all that kindness and good cooking costs an arm and a leg." He laughed again and ruffled Will's blond hair. "Just between you and me, after next week we'll be free and clear of Mrs. Clutterham."

"But she's taken care of me since Mother died," Will blurted out in surprise.

"Never mind, Willie boy," Jesse said. "You and me—we've got big adventures ahead of us. Now that the war's over, folks are moving west. Mr. Carnaby is going to turn the circus into a traveling tent show and take it on the road. He's bought gold-and-red wagons. We'll head west with the show, stopping in every town where we're sure to get a paying crowd. There'll be a big parade with our brass band leading the way. Isn't that a marvel?"

"Yes!" Will's excitement began to match his father's. "I'll help. I'll learn to do something really well. I'll make you proud of me, Fa— Jesse. I promise."

Jesse's smile disappeared. "It's hard to say this, because I'll miss you, lad. I will. But you'll not be going with me."

Will felt as if he'd been punched in the stomach. It was hard to breathe . . . hard to think. "I—I w-won't be with you? Why? Where will I go?"

"To save on expenses, we'll be traveling with a very small crew," Jesse said. "It will mostly be the entertainers and the hands needed to set up and take down the tent and feed and care for the animals."

"I can do all that," Will insisted. "I can clean cages. I can dig pits for the manure. I can sweep up."

"We're doubling up on jobs," Jesse answered. "We have no room and no money for extra help—

especially for a young boy who can't carry a full load."

Will felt a lump in his throat. But he knew his father would never forgive him if he cried. He swallowed hard and squeezed his eyes shut. "We have no relations to take me in. And you don't want me to stay with Mrs. Clutterham. Where will I go?" he asked. "What will I do?"

Once again Jesse's eyes twinkled. "I promised you an adventure, didn't I?" he asked. "You're going west, Willie, my boy! Here in New York City there is something called the Children's Aid Society. They send homeless city children on trains to towns in the West to find foster parents."

Will gasped. "I'm not homeless! I *have* a father. I have *you*."

Jesse spoke quickly, his face turning red again. "I explained to them how I'm no longer able to care for you, and they agreed to take you. Think about it, Willie. It's a grand life you'll be having. Living and working along with a family on a farm, getting plenty of fresh air and sunshine and lots of good food. And you'll be schooled for at least another two years. Now then, wouldn't you call that a wonderful adventure?"

Will ached for his mother. He had only faint memories of a gentle, loving woman who had read and sung to him. He knew his mother would never have let Jesse do this. "You're giving me away," Will whispered to Jesse. "You don't want me, so you're giving me away."

"No, no, no. You have it all wrong. It's not that I don't want you," Jesse said. "It's just that with one thing and another I can't afford to hire someone to care for you. And I can't afford to take you with me. Either way it's impossible, Willie. You see that, don't you?"

Will's throat was so tight he couldn't answer.

Jesse ruffled Will's hair again playfully. "What it comes down to is this. I'm giving you a better life," he said.

Will leaned back against the wall and closed his eyes. He couldn't speak. It was hard even to think.

"I'll come for you on Friday," Jesse said. "I'll take you to the Society and make them promise to take good care of you."

15

Will heard his father's footsteps do a *rat-tat-tat* down the porch steps and out to the sidewalk. He waited, wanting Jesse to come back and say, "Willie, I've changed my mind. I won't leave you. I can't."

After a long silence Will finally opened his eyes. The porch was empty. The street was empty. Will doubled over, pressing his head against the hard wooden bench, and cried.

CHAPTER THREE

Miss Hunter, a plump, friendly woman, led Will and Jesse into her office at the Children's Aid Society. Will huddled in his chair. He dreaded what was about to happen. He still couldn't believe his father would give him away.

"Please give me whatever forms I need to sign, so I can be on my way," Jesse told Miss Hunter. "I've got a great deal of work to finish before we leave town."

Miss Hunter looked annoyed. But her face turned sorrowful when she glanced at Will. Will stared at a picture on the wall. He didn't want anyone to pity him or to think badly of Jesse. After all, Jesse was only doing what he had to do.

Will watched as Miss Hunter dipped a pen into an open inkwell. She handed the pen and a printed sheet of paper to Jesse. Then she stood up.

"Mr. Scott, I know you want time alone to say good-bye to Will," she said.

Will watched his father quickly scrawl his name and toss down the pen.

"No need for you to leave, Miss Hunter," Jesse said. "Short good-byes are the best, don't you think?"

He shook Will's hand and grinned at him. "With luck we'll meet again someday, Willie. In the meantime, think of me now and then. Remember the fun we had. And be a good, obedient boy to your foster parents."

Will choked back a sob.

"Come, come, none of that, now." Looking uncomfortable, Jesse backed toward the door. He gave a final wave and a smile and was gone.

Miss Hunter put her arm around Will's shoulders. "Would you like to meet the other children who'll be riding the orphan train?" she asked.

It took a moment before Will was able to speak. "I'm not an orphan, and I know I'll see my father again someday," he said. The sound of his own words made him feel a little braver. "Jesse probably told you that he works for a circus—now it's a traveling tent show—but you may not know that he does trick riding, and he teaches the horses to do tricks. He's good. He's the very best."

"I'm sure he is," Miss Hunter said. "Now, why don't you come with me to meet the other children? There are some boys near your age. I'm sure they'd enjoy hearing about circus life."

Slowly Will got to his feet. He didn't want to meet the other boys. He didn't want to tell them about the circus. He didn't want to be there at all. *It's only for a short while,* he told himself. *It's only until I see my father again in the West. He'll miss me. He'll want me to come back to him. I can be patient. I can wait until then.*

Will followed Miss Hunter to a large room where thirty children were seated at tables, eating dinner.

"Scoot over, Marcus," Miss Hunter said. "Here's a boy your age—Will Scott. I know you boys will be friends."

Marcus made room for Will. The other boys at the table stared at him. They looked both wary and curious. Miss Hunter recited their names: Marcus Melo, Frank Fischer, Sam Meyer, Shane Prescott, David Howard, and Eddie Marsh. "Ask Will about his father's job," she said as she turned to leave. "Will's father is a trick rider with a circus."

Marcus's eyes narrowed with suspicion. "Never heard of a job like that," he said.

"What does a trick rider do?" David asked.

Will waited while a large bowl of vegetable soup was put on the table in front of him. Then he helped himself to two thick slices of freshly baked bread. "Jesse sometimes rides with one foot on the saddle of the lead horse and the other foot on the saddle of a second horse."

David gasped. "Two horses at one time?"

"Yes. Then he somersaults from one horse to another while they're trotting around the ring."

"You expect us to believe a story like that?" Marcus elbowed Sam, and they both snickered.

Will hesitated but then continued. "Sometimes Jesse stands on his head on the horse's saddle and fires pistols at a target."

"I'd like to see that!" David said.

The other boys burst out laughing.

"So would everybody," Marcus said. He winked at Eddie. "That's the best pack of lies I've heard all week."

"It's not a lie," Will insisted. "My father *is* a trick rider in the circus."

The boys ignored him and kept chuckling.

Silently, his face burning with hurt and anger, Will ate his supper. *Who cares what other people think?* he said to himself. *All that matters is that my father will be traveling west. And when he comes to where I'm living, he'll want me to go with him.*

From across the room Miss Hunter instructed, "When you've finished eating, children, please take your dishes to the kitchen."

Will was glad dinner was over and he could get

away from the other boys. He wished there were someplace where he could be alone. But before he could leave the dining hall, the children were gathered together and introduced to a smiling young woman named Frances Mary Kelly. Miss Kelly would be their escort on the orphan train.

She seemed friendly and kind, and she tried to talk to each of the children. But Will didn't feel like talking. All he could think about was that soon he'd be leaving New York City. He'd be leaving his father. And he'd be going to a strange place filled with people he didn't know, hoping to find someone who would take him in.

It wasn't an adventure, as Jesse had promised. It was the most frightening thing Will had ever had to do.

CHAPTER FOUR

The train ride was difficult for Will. Most of the children were orphans, and they were excited about living in real homes with new parents.

"I'll have a mother who'll tuck me in bed every night," Daisy Gordon said.

"I'll have a horse all my own," said Marcus.

"I'll go to a real school," Aggie Vaughn told them.

Lucy Griggs smiled. "I'm going to have a little sister."

But to Will each *clickety-clack* of the train's wheels meant that he was being taken farther and farther from his father. Will had desperately searched the train station for Jesse. Wouldn't he come for a last good-bye? Wouldn't he want to see Will just one more time?

Clickety-clack, clickety-clack, the wheels said. But to Will it sounded like, "You can't go back, you can't go back."

I don't have to go back. Jesse will come to get me, Will told himself. *I know he will.*

It was hard for Will to talk with the others. It was hard to keep from crying. Miss Kelly was kind, though, and Will found himself hoping his foster mother would be like her.

Harwood, Missouri, was going to be their first stop. Miss Kelly had explained that they'd leave the train and be introduced to the people who wanted foster children. Will began to wonder if he really would be chosen. His father didn't want him. What if no one else wanted him either?

Will fought his fear. He clenched his hands so tightly that his fingernails dug into his palms. He tried to imagine the town of Harwood and the people who would come to see the orphan train riders. But he couldn't.

It wasn't long until the train finally stopped in

Harwood. Miss Kelly smiled at the children. "Pick up your things, boys and girls," she said. "We'll walk two blocks to the Methodist church, where we'll meet the people who have come to see you. Remember that you're wonderful children, and I'm very, very proud of you. The families who'll get you will be lucky, so hold your heads high and smile."

People at the depot stared as Miss Kelly led the group of orphan train riders across the platform and down a dusty street to the Methodist church.

Will was surprised at how many people had come to see them. The large room they were taken to was filled. At one end of the room was a stage, and on the stage were three rows of stools. Will was led to the back row with the other older boys.

He scarcely listened as Miss Kelly gave a short talk about the Children's Aid Society and its placing-out rules. Then the children were introduced, and Miss Kelly invited people to come to the stage to talk to them. Four farmers were among the first to climb onto the stage. They went directly to the boys in the third row.

A man with a short, bristly beard ordered Marcus, "Stand up. Turn around. Let's get a good look at you."

He took hold of Marcus's wrist and lifted his arm up to make a muscle. "You look like you'll be able to handle farmwork," he said.

A stout man placed a hand on David's chin. "Open your mouth. Let's see your teeth," he said.

David did as he was told, and the man said, "Just making sure you're in good health, young man."

Will jumped as two men stepped in front of him.

The taller man shook his head. "This one's too scrawny."

But the second man said, "Might be he could fill out with a few good meals. Come over here, boy. Let's see how tall you are."

Nervously Will limped over to where the man was standing.

The two men looked at each other and shook their heads. "Got a limp, too," the tall man said. "Won't do at all."

Will backed up to his stool and sat down on it. He could have told them that the doctor had said he'd soon be able to walk without a limp. But he didn't want to go with either of these men.

Will was struck with a sudden worry. What if no one chose him here or at the other two stops? Would he be sent back to New York? And if he was, how would his father ever find him?

"Hello, young man. Will, isn't it?"

Startled, Will looked up. A gray-haired couple stood in front of him. The woman was short and plump and the man was tall and slender. Both had crinkly lines around their eyes and smiles on their lips.

"We're Sara and Otto Wallace," the woman said. "We live in Barkerville—about six miles north of Harwood. Otto's the doctor for folks in these parts." She giggled. "And sometimes he's the doctor for their animals, as well."

Dr. Wallace's voice was low and pleasant. "We've talked to Miss Kelly," he said. "She has high praise for you."

"Tell us something about yourself, Will," Mrs.

27

Wallace said. "What do you like to do? What do you like to study?"

Will thought a moment. "I'm good with reading and good with numbers," he said. "But I'm clumsy, and there's a lot of things I can't do right."

She smiled. "All boys your age are clumsy. They're all arms and legs and never know where to put their feet. There's nothing wrong with that."

Dr. Wallace spoke up. "Sara and I raised eight boys. Now all of them are grown, with families of their own."

"Except for our youngest, Roger. He's off to school in the East," Mrs. Wallace said. "We're lonely," she added. "A house isn't a home without a child in it."

"We'd like you to come and live with us, Will," Dr. Wallace said.

"Luckily, I'm a good cook." Mrs. Wallace giggled again. "It's easy to see that you're growing fast and need some meat on those bones."

Will smiled. "I *am* hungry," he said. He began to relax. He liked Dr. and Mrs. Wallace.

"Do you want to come with us?" Dr. Wallace asked again.

Will suddenly realized that he wouldn't have to go back to New York. He'd have a home with these nice people until Jesse came for him. "Yes, I do," he said eagerly. "Thank you very much."

As the Wallaces signed the papers that would put Will in their care, Will shook hands with Miss Kelly.

"Thank you for being so good to me," he said.

She put an arm around his shoulders. "Oh, Will," she answered, "I'm so happy for you. The local committee members have told me many good things about the Wallaces. You'll have a fine home with them."

Will nodded. *I probably will,* he thought. *But only until my father comes for me.*

CHAPTER FIVE

The Wallaces' home was on a road just off Barkerville's main street. Dr. and Mrs. Wallace showed Will through the two-story frame house, letting him explore the large rooms and the vegetable garden in back.

Will liked the house. The furniture was mismatched but comfortable, and there were wide windows to let in the sunlight.

Dr. Wallace proudly showed Will two rooms off the wide entry hall. One room was his office. In the other room, he examined patients.

Most of the time, however, Dr. Wallace traveled to those who needed him. "No reason to take a person out of a sickbed," he explained to Will.

During the next few days he taught Will how to hitch his old horse, Snow, to the buggy. He invited Will to assist with patients who came for help and to go along on some house calls.

Will was surprised to see that Dr. Wallace's patients often began to feel better the moment the doctor stepped into the room. Again and again he'd hear someone say, "The doctor's here. Now everything is going to be all right."

Dr. Wallace's voice was kind and soothing. He spoke to each patient calmly. He listened. And he examined every patient with care.

"Nothing broken, Zeke," he'd say. "But you're going to be a little sore for a while. If you can stay off of your leg for a few days it will heal a lot faster. Have you got some of that liniment left I gave you for your horse? Well, rub it on. It'll be just as good for you as it was for him."

Or he'd say, "Elsie, mix a spoonful of sugar with scrapings from an onion. It's the best remedy I know of for a sore throat. Stay in bed, stay warm, and you'll be feeling spry in a few days."

Dr. Wallace made a mustard plaster for Mr.

Blaine's chest to clear up his congestion. The doctor put together a flour-and-water poultice to draw the infection out of beestings on Mrs. Sommers's arm.

After each visit, on the buggy ride home, Dr. Wallace would explain to Will what he had done. And he would answer Will's questions.

Will learned a great deal just by watching Dr. Wallace at work. People were frightened when they got sick or hurt, and the first thing Dr. Wallace did was calm them down.

But sometimes Will was puzzled. "Why don't they pay you in money?" he asked. "Mrs. Root gave you a chicken and two jars of apple butter. Mrs. Blaine gave you a chicken and a dozen eggs."

"They give what they can," Dr. Wallace answered. "When the crops are in and paid for, I'm more likely to get my bills paid in cash." He grinned at Will. "In the meantime it's lucky that Sara and I are fond of chicken."

Dr. Wallace enjoyed reading. Even more, he enjoyed sharing what he read—especially items in Harwood's weekly newspaper.

One evening he grumbled, "Listen to this, Sara and Will." He indignantly rattled his paper. "President Johnson is a shortsighted, narrow-minded—"

"Now, Otto," Sara interrupted soothingly. "Calm down and just tell us what President Johnson has done this time."

Dr. Wallace read a news story about the Freedmen's Bureau, which offered aid for former slaves. The Bureau helped slaves begin new lives by giving them land and livestock, or, as they called it, "Forty Acres and a Mule." But President Johnson strongly opposed any help given to former slaves. He insisted that the former slaves should get by on their own, without help from the government. "President Johnson's a fool," Dr. Wallace snorted.

Sometimes what Dr. Wallace read would make him sadly shake his head. "Another bank near Kansas City was robbed. That makes Liberty, Lexington, and Savannah—all this year. Everyone's wondering which bank will be next. Crimes like these in peaceful communities! What is this country coming to?"

Will was relieved every time Dr. Wallace found

an item in the newspaper that pleased him. "Now, here's a man who knows what to do with his millions," Dr. Wallace said one evening. " 'The wealthy John Jay was inspired by the Louvre museum in Paris,' " he read aloud. " 'He announced that he would found a National Institution and Gallery of Art in New York City. He was promised support by other wealthy New Yorkers.' Very good. Very good. Everyone benefits from a fine museum."

Will had been with the Wallaces a little more than a month when a call came in the middle of the night. Awakened by a loud pounding at the front door, Will leaped out of bed. He heard Dr. Wallace thump down the stairs, so Will jumped into his clothes and ran downstairs after him.

"Good. You're awake," Dr. Wallace said to Will. "There was an accident at the Morleys'. Will you come with me? I could use your help."

An accident? Will wondered what kind of an accident. So far he'd only helped Dr. Wallace with sick people.

Will ran to hitch up Snow, and they raced off to the Morley farm. Dr. Wallace told Will that the boy who had come for help was named Eugene Morley and that he was the same age as Will.

"Who got hurt?" Will asked Dr. Wallace.

"Eugene's father," Dr. Wallace answered. "According to Eugene, Mr. Morley cut his leg on the blade of a scythe."

"A scythe?" Will had seen scythes—large, sharp, curved blades on poles. They were used for cutting grass and grain. "What was he doing with a scythe in the middle of the night?"

"We mend. We don't pry," Dr. Wallace said.

Will was quiet the rest of the trip. He followed Dr. Wallace into a cluttered, lantern-lit barn, where Warren Morley lay in a pool of blood. Mrs. Morley sat beside him, sobbing. Clinging to her were a half dozen frightened towheaded children. Will's nose twitched at the strange, sweet smell of blood.

Shuddering, Will backed up, his hands over his mouth. Instead of Mr. Morley, Will saw his own mother, bleeding in the street. He had wailed for his mother, terrified by the sight and the smell of her blood.

His mother had died. Was Mr. Morley going to die?

Dr. Wallace knelt at Mr. Morley's side. He pulled two clean cloths from the bag he had carried with him. One he twisted into a tourniquet, fastening it tightly above the wound on Mr. Morley's leg. Then Dr. Wallace folded the second cloth and pressed it against the wound.

"Will," he said. "Get down here. I need you to apply pressure while I get ready to take stitches."

"I . . . I . . . can't," Will whispered.

Dr. Wallace didn't even look up. In his firm, calm voice he said, "Will, I'm counting on you. Get down here. I'll show you what to do."

Trembling, Will dropped to his knees next to Dr. Wallace.

"Press firmly on this part of his leg . . . harder than that. Keep pressing. Right there," Dr. Wallace said.

Will did as he was told. He applied pressure while Dr. Wallace cleaned the wound with alcohol, threaded a long, curved needle, and began to stitch the wound together.

Mr. Morley screamed with pain and tried to kick Dr. Wallace away, but Will was stronger than the injured man. He held the wounded leg in place and kept up the pressure until Dr. Wallace told him he could stop.

After the wound was bound snugly with strips of clean, white cloth, Will, Eugene, and Dr. Wallace carried Mr. Morley into the house and put him to bed.

"Warren thought he heard a noise in the barn," Mrs. Morley told Dr. Wallace as she led the way into the kitchen. "He took a lantern and went out to look around. He must have tripped over something in the barn. I guess the scythe got knocked off its nail." She looked both angry and embarrassed as she added, "The boys are supposed to help keep the barn clean, but you know how it is. . . ."

Will glanced around the kitchen. The barn had been dirty and cluttered, and the kitchen was, too.

Eugene glared at him as he looked around. Dr. Wallace gave instructions to Mrs. Morley about changing bandages, cleaning the wound, and keeping her husband off his feet. Eugene muttered to Will, "Don't think you're better than us, Orphan Boy. You don't belong around here. You're nothin' but an orphan nobody wanted."

Eugene's words hurt, but Will didn't answer.

When Mrs. Morley thanked Dr. Wallace over and over for saving her husband's life, Dr. Wallace put a hand on Will's shoulder. "I know you'll want to thank Will, too," he said. "I would have had a hard time stopping the bleeding without Will's help."

Mrs. Morley mumbled something and busied herself wrapping up a parcel of four quarts of tomato preserves and a chicken.

"Good work, Will," Dr. Wallace said as they drove home. "You did a fine job."

The night was dark and overcast, with only a few

stars twinkling in the sky. But Will grinned as though the sun were shining. Who cared about the Morleys? He *had* done a good job. Dr. Wallace was proud of him. And Will was proud of himself.

He wished Dr. Wallace had been there when his mother had been hurt. As Snow slowly and steadily pulled the buggy toward home, Will found himself telling Dr. Wallace about his mother's accident.

"The people on the street didn't know how to stop the bleeding," he said, choking. "I was only four years old. I didn't know . . ."

"Don't blame yourself," Dr. Wallace said. "There was nothing you could have done." He placed a hand on Will's shoulder. "Look forward, Will, not back. Don't think about what might have been. Think about what *can* be. Now that you know what to do, you might be able to save someone else's life someday."

They had nearly reached the barn before Will spoke again. "I like going to visit patients with you," he said. "I watch what you do and listen to what you say. I'm learning a lot of things I never even thought about before."

CHAPTER SIX

Will worked hard, volunteering for any job that needed doing around the house. He especially liked taking care of Mrs. Wallace's vegetable garden. But there was one task he hated. He used every excuse he could think of to avoid going with Mrs. Wallace on her shopping trips to town.

Whenever Will walked down the main street of Barkerville with Mrs. Wallace, people stared and whispered. But what Will hated the most was having to face the two-story building just past the blacksmith shop, post office, bank, and stores. It was Barkerville's meeting hall and schoolhouse.

"You haven't met many children yet," Mrs. Wallace told Will. "But just wait until school is open in September. It will be good for you to make friends with boys your age."

Will thought about Eugene's unfriendly words. But it wasn't just Eugene Will was worried about. Dr. Wallace had introduced Will to some boys his age after church services, but they had just stared at him.

"Dirty little orphan," one of them had mumbled.

"Never knew his father," another had whispered.

"Found in a gutter, just like Eugene told us," a third boy had said, snickering.

Angry and hurt, Will had wanted to explain that he *wasn't* an orphan, that he had a father. But the boys had run off for a game of kickball, ignoring him.

From that time on, Will had been careful to avoid the boys his age. When school began, though, he wouldn't be able to avoid them.

Mrs. Wallace's voice broke into Will's thoughts.

"You're going to love all the wonderful parties that are held in the schoolhouse, Will. I can't wait until they start up again in September."

When Will didn't respond, she said, "We'll have box suppers and talent shows and spelling bees." She smiled proudly. "For five years our Roger took first place in the spelling bees."

Will cringed at the thought. He'd been in a spelling bee back in New York. He'd stood in line with the other boys and girls in his class. Their parents had crowded into the small seats and watched closely. Will had searched the room for Jesse as the words were called out. At first the words had been simple, and Will had spelled his easily.

Where is Jesse? Will had wondered. *He promised to come.*

The spelling words had grown longer and harder, but Will had no trouble with them. One after another, his schoolmates missed words and had to sit down. But not Will. He knew he had a chance to win. Spelling was something he was good at, and he had badly wanted Jesse to be there to see and hear him.

But where was Jesse?

Just as Will's turn had come, Jesse had bounced through the door. He'd leaned against the back wall, grinning and waving at Will.

With a great sigh of relief, Will had waved back.

Robert, who stood next to Will, had jabbed him with his elbow. Will suddenly became aware that the caller had spoken to him.

"I'm sorry, sir. I didn't hear the word," Will had said.

"Words cannot be repeated. I must follow the rules," the caller had told him, frowning. "You have five more seconds."

There was nothing Will could do but stand there, his palms wet and his face burning with embarrassment. He hadn't heard the word. The seconds had ticked by, and the caller had said, "Time." Will was out of the spelling bee.

"Equinox." The caller repeated the word, and Robert spelled it easily.

Will had groaned. *I knew that word,* he thought. *I would have got it right.* He glanced at his father, miserable at the disappointment he saw on Jesse's face.

Later Jesse had told him, "Don't worry about it, Willie. Someday we'll find something you can do well." He'd laughed as he added, "We haven't found it yet, but so help me, we'll keep trying."

"Will? Will?" Mrs. Wallace stopped short so suddenly that Will tripped, trying not to run into her. "I don't believe you've heard a thing I've been saying."

"I heard," Will answered. "You were talking about a spelling bee."

She smiled. "You'll enjoy entering the spelling bees."

Will quickly shook his head. "I couldn't win a spelling bee. I'm not smart like Roger. Isn't he the one who's at the university in Boston?"

"Yes, he is. And you're every bit as smart as Roger," Mrs. Wallace said. She tilted her head as she studied Will's face. "You've got a good mind.

Otto tells me you're quick to learn, and you're a great help with his patients. Hasn't anyone ever told you how smart you are?"

"No," Will said. He knew that Mrs. Wallace was just being kind.

"Well, they should have told you, because you are," Mrs. Wallace insisted.

Will just shrugged and followed her into the dry goods store.

Across the room, where bolts of cotton cloth lay in bright rows, Will spotted Eugene with his mother.

Mrs. Morley's eyes lit up when she spied Mrs. Wallace. She hurried over, Eugene dragging his feet as he followed her.

"Sara," Mrs. Morley cried, "I haven't had a chance to talk to you since Warren's accident!"

Mrs. Wallace hugged Mrs. Morley as she chattered about dangerous scythes and the terrible accidents they could cause. "We're so thankful that Warren has recovered so well," Mrs. Morley said. "Warren's always so careful. We just can't imagine how the accident happened."

Will glanced at Eugene, whose face was red with embarrassment. He remembered Dr. Wallace's words, "We mend. We don't pry."

Eugene glared back at Will, his mouth twisting down in anger. *He thinks I'm going to say that the barn was a mess and that's why the accident happened,* Will thought.

"Otto's a good doctor," Mrs. Morley was saying. She smiled. "And you're a good cook, Sara. Thank you for sending over the soup."

Mrs. Wallace put a hand on Will's shoulder. "I understand that Will was a big help in patching up Warren. Otto told me he didn't know what he would have done without Will's fine help."

Looking surprised, Mrs. Morley glanced at Will for the first time. "Oh, the orphan boy. Yes, he was on hand. I tell you, I was so frightened, Sara, I didn't much pay attention to anything except what the doctor was doing."

Will felt the pressure of Mrs. Wallace's fingers on his shoulder. He knew she was angry. Her voice, though, remained calm and pleasant as she said, "Will is part of our family now, Edna. I'm

47

glad you can meet him under these happier conditions."

Mrs. Morley took another, more curious look at Will and nodded.

Mrs. Wallace looked pointedly at Eugene. "I'm sure you and Will are going to become friends once school starts. You should both be in the same grade, seventh. Am I right?"

When neither Eugene nor his mother answered, Mrs. Wallace sighed. "Come along, Will, and help me pick out some cloth you like. I have a mind to make you a new shirt."

As Will passed Eugene in the aisle, Eugene put out a foot to stop him. "Just watch out, Orphan Boy," he muttered in a low voice. "You're gonna get what's coming to you."

CHAPTER SEVEN

The school year began as soon as the crops were harvested in September. On the first day of school the weather shifted, and there was a chill bite to the air.

Mrs. Wallace hunted through some clothes packed away in the attic until she found a heavy wool jacket that would fit Will. "This was Gerald's," she said. "He was a few years older than you, Will, when he wore it. It's hard to believe how much taller and stronger you've grown since you came to us."

I really am getting taller and stronger, Will thought, and his heart leaped with excitement. *I'll be big and strong enough to help my father when he comes this way with the tent show. He'll want to take me with him. I know he will.*

Mrs. Wallace packed Will a lunch of sandwiches and apples. She tucked them into a blue-and-white tin bucket with the name WALLACE painted on the lid. "This was Henry's," she said. "It has a few dents, but no one will care. Only the little ones start school with new lunch buckets."

Dr. Wallace solemnly shook Will's hand. "I'm glad you're getting an education, Will, but I'll miss your help," he said.

"I'll be here after school to help you," Will offered.

Mrs. Wallace shook her head. "Homework comes first," she told him.

Will felt disappointed and said, "I can still go on calls with you."

"Not if they're late at night," Mrs. Wallace replied. "You'll need your rest."

Dr. Wallace grinned. "We'll work something out, Will. I don't want to lose my assistant. You've got a real knack for helping sick folks."

Will enjoyed the pride and happiness that bubbled up inside him. But he pushed the feelings away. *How can you become a part of a family you don't really belong to?* he asked himself. *How can you do that to Jesse?*

Kissing Will's forehead, Mrs. Wallace told him, "Have a good day at school, Will." But she didn't let go of his shoulders. She looked into his eyes as she said, "I hope you'll make good friends—with boys you'll enjoy growing up with. Sometimes it's hard at first, but keep in mind that Dr. Wallace and I are proud of you. We love you, Will."

Will couldn't speak. He hugged Mrs. Wallace. Then he turned and ran down the road to Main Street. Guilt rose like a hard, painful lump in his throat. Dr. and Mrs. Wallace were the kindest, nicest people he had ever met. He couldn't tell them that he didn't care if he made friends or not. Making friends didn't matter, because he was not going to grow up with the boys in Barkerville. As soon as Carnaby's Traveling Tent Show arrived, Will was leaving with his father.

As Will came near the school, he saw Eugene and some of his friends standing near the stairs that led to the front door of the building.

"Orphan Boy," Eugene taunted. "Never had a mother or a father. Nobody wanted him."

The other boys laughed, but Will didn't turn around. He walked through the big double doors into a wide hallway. There were open doors on each side that led into two rooms filled with neat rows of desks and chairs. Ahead of him was another set of double doors, but they were closed. Mrs. Wallace had mentioned a large community meeting room. Maybe the meeting room was behind the double doors.

Will walked to the doorway on his left and looked inside. Behind a large desk sat a very young woman with her hair pinned up in a bun. She looked up and smiled at Will.

"Good morning," she said. "I'm Miss Davis. Are you a new student?"

"Yes," Will said. "I'm Will Scott."

She smiled again. "You want Mr. Schultz's room, across the hallway. I teach grades one through four. He teaches the students in grades five through eight."

Only two rooms? Will wondered. This school was going to be very different from the large one he was used to in New York City.

"Thank you," Will said to Miss Davis. He walked to the other room and stopped in front of Mr. Schultz's desk.

Mr. Schultz was a middle-aged, balding man with wire-rimmed glasses perched crookedly on his nose. He leaned back in his chair and looked up at Will.

"Mr. Schultz, I'm Will Scott. I'm a new student. I live with Dr. and Mrs. Wallace," Will said.

Mr. Schultz leaned his elbows on his desk and peered at Will with interest. "So . . . you're the boy who came on the orphan train," he said.

Will took a deep breath. "I'm not an orphan," he answered. "I have a father. He sent me to find a new home because he couldn't take care of me any longer."

Mr. Schultz pushed his chair back and got to his feet. He wasn't a tall man, but he seemed very big to Will. "Well, the first thing to do is see where you fit in. How old are you?"

"Twelve."

"Can you read?"

"Yes, sir."

Mr. Schultz picked up a book of essays and handed it to Will. "Open it anywhere and read aloud," he said.

Will did it easily.

"Very good," Mr. Schultz said. "Have you studied American history?"

"Yes," Will answered.

"Who's the current president of the United States?"

That was easy, too. "Andrew Johnson," Will said.

"How many presidents have we had before President Johnson?"

Will didn't hesitate. "Sixteen. Andrew Johnson is our seventeenth president."

Mr. Schultz's eyes twinkled. "Can you name them all?"

Will took another long breath and began.

"George Washington, John Adams . . ." He almost mixed up Presidents Tyler and Taylor, but straightened them out, getting James K. Polk in the right place between them.

Mr. Schultz nodded. "The Thirteenth Amendment to the United States Constitution was signed last year. Do you know its purpose?"

"Yes, sir," Will answered. "It abolished slavery."

"How many states are there in the United States?"

"Thirty-six." Will smiled. This was simple.

"I'm going to put you in the seventh grade," Mr. Schultz said. "Some of the work may be too easy for you, but some lessons will take hard study. I'm sure you can meet the challenge."

Mr. Schultz picked up a large handbell and held the clapper to keep it silent. "Put your things in the cloakroom in the back. Then take the third seat in the row by the window," he said. He smiled. "And watch out for the mob that's going to race in here the moment I ring this bell."

Will quickly hung up his jacket and put his lunch bucket on the shelf. He took his seat and waited. His mouth was dry and his palms were sweaty.

He heard the loud clanging of the bell and the thundering rush of footsteps up the outside stairs. Miss Davis kept calling out, "Children, form a single line. Walk. Do not run. Form a single line, please."

Maybe the boys and girls in Miss Davis's class paid attention to her, Will thought, but Mr. Schultz's students didn't. He watched them dash through the lobby of the building and into the classroom.

Some of them stopped talking when they saw Will. All of them eyed him carefully. Will clutched the edge of the desk and stared back.

Suddenly Eugene stood next to him. "You're in my seat," he said. "Get out."

Will looked up. "I'm sitting where Mr. Schultz told me to sit."

"No, you're not. You're too stupid to know where to sit. I told you to get out of my seat."

Will looked around for Mr. Schultz, but he wasn't in the classroom. "But—" Will began.

Before he could say another word, someone grabbed his collar, jerking him out of his seat. Will landed on the floor on his hands and knees, wincing as the toe of a boot jabbed his leg.

As Will struggled to get to his feet, he was aware of a sudden quiet in the room. Everyone was seated except for Mr. Schultz, who walked across the room to stand in front of Will.

"What happened?" Mr. Schultz asked quietly.

A boy seated across the aisle spoke up. "The orphan started a fight," he said.

"You saw this, Elmer?"

"Yes, sir."

Will recognized Elmer. He was a friend of Eugene's. He looked at Elmer and Elmer stared back, a smirk on his face.

"If there was a fight, then with whom was Will fighting? It takes at least two to have a fight."

Elmer's smirk disappeared. He didn't answer.

Mr. Schultz waited only a moment. Then he said, "Will, I assigned you a seat. Why don't you sit in it?"

Eugene sprawled across the double bench of the desk. "It's *my* seat."

"You'll both fit," Mr. Schultz said. "Move over, Eugene, and give Will some room."

"My ma won't like it, you putting me with the orphan who doesn't even know who his parents were," Eugene grumbled.

"I'm *not* an orphan," Will said loudly. "I have a father."

"That's a lie," Eugene said. "I know what my pa and ma told me. You orphans from New York were born in gutters, and none of you know who your fathers were."

Will clenched his teeth. "I told you, I have a father."

"Oh, yeah?" Eugene sneered. "Prove it!"

CHAPTER EIGHT

More than anything else Will wanted to prove to Eugene and the others that he had a father. There was only one way. Carnaby's Traveling Tent Show—starring Jesse Scott—would have to come to town. But Will had so much work to do, he didn't have time to think about it.

Will worked hard both at school and at home. He liked learning, and he liked Mr. Schultz. Eugene and Elmer kept saying mean things to him about orphans, but Will tried his best to ignore them.

A few of the boys and girls in Mr. Schultz's class seemed friendly. Pudgy Arthur Banks, who couldn't shoot a marble straight, began sitting next to Will at lunchtime. Susie Chatham always smiled at Will. But Will reminded himself that he wasn't interested in making friends. Not when he'd soon be leaving town with Jesse.

The fall weather was sunny and crisp, and each day Will hoped to discover that Carnaby's Traveling Tent Show was on its way. He eagerly read the notices tacked to the storefronts in town. But Will was disappointed when he saw they were only advertisements for a land sale near Harwood or a store's new supply of ladies' hats.

Where were Jesse and the circus?

One day in school, Mr. Schultz announced that a spelling bee was scheduled for October. "I'll give each of you a list of words, and I want you to study," he said. "All your parents will be there."

Eugene's elbow suddenly jabbed into Will's ribs. "You haven't got a chance, Orphan Boy," Eugene whispered. "I came in second last year. This year I'm going to win."

Will was swept by a strong desire to beat him. "Think again," he told Eugene. "This is going to be one more year when you *won't* win."

On the evening of the spelling bee the meeting hall was packed with people from miles around, all dressed in their best outfits. Mrs. Wallace had spent hours drilling Will in his spelling. When they entered the hall, she turned to him and said, "I'm so proud of you."

Will wiped his sweating hands on his pants. "What if I make a mistake? What if I forget the words? What if—?"

Mrs. Wallace hugged him. "I'd still be proud of you for studying well and trying your best. Just between you and me, though, I think you can win."

Then the crowd was hushed, the caller was introduced, and the students formed two lines.

Everyone stayed in during the first round. But as the words grew harder, the younger students dropped out quickly. Finally the only spellers left were Arthur Banks, Susie Chatham, Emily Jones, Eugene Morley, and Will.

The Wallaces smiled at Will and nodded encouragement. But Mr. and Mrs. Morley sat stone-faced. Mr. Morley gripped his hands together so tightly his knuckles looked like white knobs.

"Antecedence," the caller said to Emily.

"A-n-t-i-c-e-d-e-n-c-e," Emily said.

"That is incorrect," the caller said, and looked at Arthur. *"Antecedence,"* he pronounced carefully.

"A-n-t-e-s-e-e-d-e-n-c-e," Arthur spelled.

"Incorrect," the caller announced. Will was next. *"Antecedence."*

Will took a deep breath and pictured the word in his mind. *"A-n-t-e-c-e-d-e-n-c-e,"* he said.

"Correct," the caller said.

Will heard Mr. Morley grumble, "That orphan has no business being in here with our children."

Embarrassed, Will looked away. He hoped no one else had heard what Mr. Morley had said.

Susie went down on the word *penurious,* but Will spelled it correctly.

There were just two contestants left, Will and Eugene.

"Somniferous," the caller said. Will spelled it correctly.

"Triptych . . . vigesimal . . . insurgency." The

words came quickly. Will and Eugene spelled them easily.

But then it was Eugene's turn, and the word was *solstitial.*

"Huh?" Eugene said. "That word wasn't on the list."

"Yes, it was," Mr. Schultz said.

"You have five seconds," the caller told Eugene.

Will watched as Eugene's face turned red and his hands balled into tight fists. *"S-o-l-s-t-i-s-h-a-l,"* Eugene spelled.

"That is incorrect," the caller said. He looked at Will. *"Solstitial,"* he said.

"S-o-l-s-t-i-t-i-a-l," Will spelled.

"Correct," the caller announced. "Will Scott has won the spelling bee."

The audience applauded. Mrs. Wallace jumped to her feet, smiling and clapping her hands. Dr. Wallace grinned proudly. But Will saw Mr. Morley roughly grab Eugene's arm. "What's the matter with you?" he snapped. "Why'd you let that orphan boy beat you?"

Will saw the hurt on Eugene's face, and for a

moment he felt sorry for him. But Mrs. Wallace had made her way to the front of the room and was hugging Will. Dr. Wallace shouted "Congratulations!" and clapped him on the back.

This is the way Jesse would have acted if I'd won that other spelling bee, Will thought. *Jesse would have clapped and cheered. Jesse would have been just as excited as the Wallaces . . . wouldn't he?*

The Thanksgiving holiday passed, and soon after, a cold front swept across Missouri. "Maybe we'll have snow for Christmas," Mrs. Wallace said. "Wouldn't that be nice?"

"It would be nice to have strawberries for dessert," Dr. Wallace said.

"Strawberries? In winter?"

"I read that a man in Detroit has just built a refrigerated, ice-cooled freight car. He claims it can be used to ship fresh fruit and vegetables from one end of the country to the other."

"Ridiculous!" exclaimed Mrs. Wallace in disbelief. "You certainly don't need ice cooling in wintertime."

"I'm just telling you what I read," Dr. Wallace said. "There's another inventor, this one in Illinois, who is going to use ice cooling too. He plans to ship strawberries by rail from warmer climates to colder ones in wintertime. He said he'd charge customers two dollars a quart."

Mrs. Wallace rolled her eyes. "That's the most foolish thing I ever heard of. Who in their right minds would pay two dollars for strawberries? Answer me that!"

"I'm not arguing with you," Dr. Wallace tried to explain. "I'm just telling you what I read in the newspaper. It's important to read, isn't it, son?" he said to Will, ruffling his hair.

"Yes, sir," Will replied.

Will gave up hoping that Carnaby's Traveling Tent Show would soon come to town. He knew that the circus would stay in one place during the cold winter months when it was impossible to travel. Will's days were busy, but each night, before he fell asleep, he thought about his father.

Where are you, Jesse? he'd ask, trying in the darkness to picture his father's face. *Are you sorry now that you gave me away? Do you miss me as much as I miss you?* Will tried to stop thinking about his father, but he couldn't.

Christmas was hard for Will. Christmas was for families—families like the Wallaces. Five of the Wallace children came home for the holidays. Four of them brought their wives and children. The house was filled with laughter and plump babies, and everyone was kind to Will.

"Welcome to the family," Gerald said. He put an arm around Will's shoulders.

"You're just what we needed—another brother," Roger said, and everyone laughed, even Will.

Still, it was impossible for Will to relax and think of the Wallaces as his family. Jesse was his family and always would be. But now and then Will wondered if he'd ever see his father again.

On Christmas morning there was a stocking full of gifts for each member of the Wallace household.

Will poured out the contents of his stocking and

found two oranges, a handful of walnuts and pecans in their shells, and twists of homemade taffy. There was also a pocketknife in a bone case. It was so beautiful that Will whistled when he saw it.

Dr. Wallace smiled. "I figured you'd like it, son."

Will's heart gave a jump and he fought back the tears that burned his eyes. Could he be a son to both Dr. Wallace and Jesse? Taking a breath to steady himself, Will said, "I do like the knife! Thank you!" He held the knife on his palm, stroking the smooth case with one finger and wondering what Jesse would think of his gift.

Mrs. Wallace and her daughters-in-law spent most of the day in the kitchen. The mingled fragrances of roast beef, rich gravy, and sweet potato pie made Will so hungry he could hardly stand it.

"Come to dinner!" Mrs. Wallace finally called.

Will's mouth watered when he saw all the bowls heaped with colorful vegetables, spicy stewed fruits, and creamy potatoes.

"Otto, will you say the blessing?" Mrs. Wallace asked.

But before Dr. Wallace could open his mouth, a loud hammering at the front door made them all jump.

Will ran to open the door. There stood a man so bundled against the cold that Will didn't recognize him. A gust of white flakes blew in the door with him.

"Doc!" the man cried. "It's me—Luke Jonah. The wife's taken sick. She's in a lot of pain, way down in her stomach. I'm scared for her, Doc!"

Dr. Wallace was already reaching for his hat, coat, gloves, and muffler. "You go ahead, Luke," he said. "I'll catch up."

Will gave a last, longing glance at the table. He couldn't let Dr. Wallace go alone in weather like this. "I'll go with you," he said, and ran to get his coat.

In the buggy, Dr. Wallace hunched over Snow's reins. "I appreciate your coming with me," he said. "I know your mouth was watering for all that good food the ladies set on the table."

As if in answer, Will's stomach rumbled loudly. Both of them laughed.

For a while they rode in silence. Then Dr. Wallace said, "I hope you'll give some thought to someday studying medicine. You're an intelligent, responsible young man. I think you have a real knack for taking care of people."

Even though Will felt a jolt of excitement at the idea of someday becoming a doctor, he shook his head. "I *have* thought about it, Dr. Wallace. I do like helping sick people get better. And I like watching and learning from you. But studying medicine isn't for me."

Dr. Wallace looked sharply at Will. "Why not?"

"Because . . . because . . ." In spite of the cold, Will felt his face burn. He couldn't tell Dr. Wallace about his plan to find his father and go with him again.

Dr. Wallace smiled and gave a flick to the reins. "Don't worry about how your education will be paid for, if that's what's bothering you," he said. "If you want to become a doctor, Sara and I will make sure that you have what you need."

Will squirmed, even more embarrassed and miserable. He thought only about Jesse and about being with him again. No matter how close he felt to Dr. Wallace, Will couldn't share this secret with him.

CHAPTER NINE

In early spring, crocuses and daffodils poked through the newly thawed earth. The walls and windows of Barkerville were papered with a new flock of notices.

Will stopped in front of the printed sheet of paper fastened to the front of the dry goods store. As he read, he caught his breath. The words began to blur before his eyes.

The Carnaby Traveling Tent Show! Jesse was coming to Harwood!

Will's heart pounded, but he forced himself to calm down. The tent show would set up on Rankin Road, just outside Barkerville. *Only six miles away!* Will thought. There'd be a Saturday-morning parade through downtown Harwood, followed by an evening performance. On Sunday, both an afternoon and evening performance would be given. Then the show would close up and move on.

Jesse! Jesse's coming! Over and over Will read the best part of the notice—his father's name, printed in large letters. JESSE SCOTT. RINGMASTER AND WORLD-FAMOUS TRICK RIDER.

Will ran the rest of the way to school. Soon he'd see his father! Will imagined the admiration he'd see in his father's eyes. Jesse would take one look at him and say, "Look how you've grown and filled out."

"I can do the work of any man," Will would tell him. "I want to go with you."

Jesse would answer, "I want you to come. I've missed you."

And Will would be able to prove to Eugene that he had a father.

"Will!" a familiar voice called excitedly, and his daydream disappeared. "Will, did you see that a tent show is coming to Harwood?"

Will turned and saw Arthur Banks. "Yes," he answered.

Arthur's eyes widened. "I've never seen a circus. Have you?"

Will opened his mouth to tell Arthur about Jesse, then thought better of it. He'd have to tell Dr. and Mrs. Wallace first, unless . . .

Maybe I shouldn't tell them, he thought. The Wallaces had signed some papers for Will. Maybe it meant that he *had* to stay with them. If so, he couldn't go with Jesse.

"Well, have you?" Arthur repeated.

"Uh . . . yes, I have," Will answered.

"Oh. In New York City?"

"That's right."

"Lucky you," Arthur said. "Wanna go with me and my family Saturday morning to see the parade?"

"Sure. Thanks," Will said calmly. But his heart was beating fast with excitement.

Susie Chatham smiled at Will as he reached the stairs. "I'm going to the parade with my parents," she said. "If you want, you can ride with us."

Just then Mr. Schultz appeared at the top of the stairs and rang the school bell. "Settle down," he called. "Settle down. I know you're all excited about the tent show, but you've got lessons to learn."

Will hurried up the stairs. It was going to be awfully hard to wait until Saturday.

That evening at supper Will gave up trying to work the tent show into the conversation. He finally blurted out, "Arthur and I would like to go to Harwood on Saturday to see the circus parade. Arthur asked me to go with his family. Susie Chatham asked me too, but I'd rather go with Arthur."

Mrs. Wallace and Dr. Wallace exchanged a quick glance before she answered. "So that's why you've been wiggling and squirming and not eating more than a few bites of your supper. You've got the circus on your mind."

Dr. Wallace looked up from his plate of baked chicken. Will held his breath. He hadn't told Dr. or Mrs. Wallace that his father was with Carnaby's

Traveling Tent Show. And he couldn't say anything now—not with the plans he'd made.

Dr. Wallace smiled. "If you want to go to the parade with Arthur, it's fine with us," he said. He smiled and added, "By the way, I'm going to get our tickets for the Saturday-night performance."

"Wonderful!" Mrs. Wallace said. "I'd love to see the circus." When Will didn't speak up, she looked at him curiously and asked, "You want to see it too, don't you, Will?"

"Oh, yes!" Will answered quickly. "Thank you, Mrs. Wallace. Thank you, Dr. Wallace."

Will got the uneasy feeling that they were waiting for him to say more, but he didn't know what else he could say. He only hoped neither of them could hear the rapid beating of his heart.

CHAPTER TEN

Each day Will tried to keep his mind on his studies, and he worked hard at his chores. But all he really wanted to think about was seeing his father again on Saturday.

Will's stomach hurt from nervous excitement, and he found it hard to eat. On Saturday he'd find out what his future would be. Surely Jesse would want him back. Or would he? Jesse would ask Will to leave with him and the tent show, unless . . .

Of course he will, Will told himself. *He has to.*

Somehow Will managed to get through the days, and finally it was Saturday. But Arthur's family was late to pick Will up, and their horse was slow. The parade had already turned onto the main street of Harwood by the time Will and Arthur could jump from the Bankses' wagon and squeeze their way through the crowd.

A small brass band led the way, followed by six elegant gold-and-red wagons. The performers, in their colorful costumes, rode high on top of the wagons. They waved to both sides as they passed by.

Inside one of the wagons, behind bars, Gorgo, the trained bear, paced and growled. Susie, standing in the front row, screamed and clutched her mother.

The lions rode in the next wagon. They looked sleepy and bored to Will. Nevertheless parents held tightly to their children, who squealed with excitement. Will realized that most of the people watching the parade had never seen a lion—especially up close.

The trim circus horses, their manes decorated with ribbon rosettes and streamers, trotted along next. On the back of one of the horses—dressed in a spangled coat and tights—rode Jesse.

"Jesse!" Will shouted, but the loud calliope that

brought up the rear of the parade drowned out Will's voice.

Will waved both arms, but Jesse didn't see him.

Suddenly, Jesse stood on the rump of his horse. In one swift motion he leaped onto the back of another horse and waved to the crowd.

Over the loud music Will cupped his hands and shouted, "Jesse, it's me! I'm here!" But Jesse still didn't hear or see him.

Soon Jesse had passed by and Will stepped back, heartsick. *He didn't even look for me,* he said to himself. He thought about the day he had climbed on board the orphan train and how he had searched the crowd at the depot, hoping with all his heart to see his father one more time. Why didn't Jesse look for him?

"Hey, Will," Arthur said. "What's the matter with you? I asked if you want to go to the store with me and get a taffy twist." He held his palm out flat. "Ma gave me some pennies."

Will looked around, surprised. The crowd was

drifting away. "No, thanks," he said. "Arthur, I'm not riding back home with your family. I'm going to watch the circus people set up the tent."

"You can't," Arthur said. "My pa told me they won't allow anyone on the grounds till they're ready for tonight's show."

"It's okay," Will said. "I'll stay out of the way."

"But won't Mrs. Wallace expect you back home?"

"No. I told Dr. Wallace I'd meet them at the ticket booth right before tonight's show." Will felt guilty, knowing he'd let the Wallaces think he'd be with Arthur's family. *But I don't have a choice,* he told himself. *I have to talk to my father.*

"I'll see you later," Will called to Arthur. He walked away, then broke into a run, heading for the circus lot.

When he arrived, a tall, muscular man moved toward him. "No one allowed here. You could get hurt. You'll have to—" He stopped, looking puzzled. Then he broke into a wide, gap-toothed grin. "Is that you, Will Scott?"

"It's me, Henry." Will remembered the circus hand well. "I've come to see my father."

"He'll be surprised." Henry motioned toward the wagons. "Go ahead, Will. You'll find Jesse changing his costume."

Will saw two men come out of one of the wagons, so he knew that was the men's dressing room. He ran up the wooden steps and opened the door.

Jesse, now dressed in work clothes, was leaning into a mirror, smiling as he combed his hair.

"Fa— Jesse!" Will cried.

Jesse whirled around and stared. Then he began to laugh. "Willie, boy!" he shouted. "Is it really you?"

"It's me," Will said. His eyes blurred with happy tears.

"Now, now. None of that baby stuff." Jesse strode to Will and clutched his shoulders, looking him up and down. "You've grown. Look how tall and filled out you are."

"I'm strong, too," Will told him. "Give me a job with the circus. I want to come with you."

Jesse was quiet for a moment while Will held his breath.

Finally he spoke. "Well, why not?" Jesse said. "It would mean another paycheck for us. I'll talk to Mr. Carnaby. He'll have use for another hand. I'm sure of it."

Will was so excited he could hardly stand it. Jesse wanted him!

Jesse sat on a nearby stool and pointed to another one, motioning Will to be seated. "We've got a few minutes to talk before I tend to the horses. So tell me, Willie, what have you been up to?"

"I've been living with Dr. and Mrs. Wallace," Will answered. "They take good care of me. I go with Dr. Wallace on his house calls and help him take care of people who are sick and hurt. One time—"

"I'll bet that fine doctor hasn't paid you a cent for all your hard work," Jesse said.

"Well, no, but—"

"Enough about him. I know you want to hear about the circus and how well it's doing," Jesse said. "We keep drawing big crowds. Carnaby's added some more animals. He's hired a sword swallower, four trapeze artists, and a woman bareback rider—a bit daring, but we've had no complaints. And he's put my name in big letters. Have you seen the notices?"

"Yes," Will said.

"Then you've seen how important Carnaby thinks I am. Best rider in the country! You should have seen my performances in St. Louis, where we spent the winter. We drew big crowds." Jesse suddenly jumped to his feet. "How'd you like to give me some help right now? You know what's needed in caring for the horses."

Eager to help, Will stumbled as he scrambled up, knocking over the stool.

Jesse smiled and shook his head. "Still clumsy, Willie boy? I thought you'd outgrow that."

"Mrs. Wallace says that all boys—"

Dropping his voice, Jesse said, "Listen, Willie. There's no need to bother the folks who've taken care of you by telling them that you're leaving. Who knows? They might come up with a bill for the things they've given you, and I'm a little short of cash right now. They'd probably overcharge anyway, like Mrs. Clutterham did." He chuckled. "Slipped out on her, we did, and it served her right."

"But—"

"No buts about it. Here's our plan. We'll put on our shows tonight and tomorrow. Then we'll pack up and be on the road. Be here, Willie boy, by eleven o'clock tomorrow night. You can ride on the second wagon with me."

The rest of the day passed in a happy blur as Will worked beside his father and ate with the other circus employees. They didn't know yet, but Will would soon be one of them again.

The performance that evening was better than it had ever been. The audience shouted and cheered for each of the acts. Will sat squeezed between Dr. and Mrs. Wallace on one of the hard benches. He shouted and applauded with everyone else. But his mind wasn't on the circus. All he could think about was going away with Jesse.

After the show, on the way home in the buggy, Mrs. Wallace went over the acts, describing them again and again. She talked as though Dr. Wallace and Will hadn't seen them. She spoke so quickly that her voice shook, and Will saw her hands trembling. She reminded Will of a clock that had been wound up and couldn't stop. *What is the matter with her?* Will wondered. *Why can't she stop talking?*

Will and Dr. Wallace just listened. But as soon as they'd arrived home and climbed the stairs, Dr. Wallace followed Will into his bedroom. "Is there anything you'd like to talk about, son?" he asked.

Will gulped. He couldn't meet Dr. Wallace's eyes. "No," he said. "Nothing."

"If there ever is," Dr. Wallace said, "don't hesitate to come to us. Sara and I are always here to help you."

Will was glad when Dr. Wallace left and shut the door behind him. Will flopped onto the bed, groaning, his excitement mingled with misery.

Dr. and Mrs. Wallace are kind and loving, Will

thought. *They care about me, and I care about them. It's going to hurt them when I leave with Jesse.*

Will squirmed onto his side, then rolled onto his back, unable to find a comfortable position. *They're not my real family,* he told himself. *Jesse is. And Jesse wants me back. He really does.*

CHAPTER ELEVEN

Sunday was pure torment for Will. After church services he worked in the garden until he was exhausted. He hoped that hard work would keep him from having to think about what he was planning to do. But the work didn't help. The hours dragged by until bedtime finally came.

Will went to bed with all his clothes on. He heard Mrs. Wallace come up the stairs. She peeked in, checking to see that he was all right. With the blankets pulled up to his ears, Will pretended to be asleep. Mrs. Wallace waited a few moments; then Will heard her shut the door.

A little later he heard Dr. Wallace wind the

clock, then slowly climb the stairs. Once again Will's door opened, and he knew Dr. Wallace was watching him. Will breathed evenly, hoping Dr. Wallace would believe he was asleep.

The door closed quietly, and Will lay awake, staring into the moonlit room. He waited impatiently for the clock to strike ten-thirty.

When it did, Will silently slid open his bedroom window and slipped outside. He swung onto a branch of a nearby tree and climbed down. Taking only the clothes he was wearing, he ran down the road in the darkness toward Harwood. He hoped he would arrive there in time.

He was getting close to Harwood when someone dashed out of the lane that led to the Morleys' farm. The dark figure ran straight at Will and gripped his arms.

Will let out a yelp and punched at the person.

"Stop! It's me, Eugene!" a voice yelled. Eugene leaned against Will, wheezing and panting for breath. "My little brother Amos . . . the ax . . . he's bad hurt . . . the horse is sick . . . I've got to run for the doctor." Eugene clutched Will's shoulders. "You've got to help Amos, Will."

"You don't need me. You need Dr. Wallace," Will said.

"I need both of you," Eugene insisted. "You can get to my house first. Ma doesn't know how to stop the bleeding. She's just screaming and hollering, and Pa's so angry he's just yelling at everybody."

"You have to put on a tourniquet and apply pressure until the doctor gets there," Will said.

"Don't tell me. Tell Ma," Eugene shouted as he turned and ran toward the Wallaces'. "I'm going for the doctor."

Will took a couple of steps toward Harwood. By this time the tents would be down and packed. Lanterns would be wobbling back and forth across the empty field, and the large circus wagons would already be hitched. Jesse would be waiting for him.

But the Morleys needed help and needed it right now. Into Will's mind came the picture of his mother, lying bleeding in the street with no one who knew how to help her.

"I can't!" Will groaned. "I have to go with Jesse!" But Will pictured little Amos with his missing front teeth and funny grin. He turned and ran as fast as he could up the lane toward the Morleys' house.

Mrs. Morley sat on the ground wailing loudly. Mr. Morley, his face twisted with worry, knelt by Amos. He looked up when he saw Will and asked gruffly, "Where's the doctor?"

"He's coming," Will said. "I'll help Amos until Dr. Wallace gets here."

Mr. Morley got out of the way, and Will knelt next to the little boy. He tore the sleeve of Amos's shirt away from the wound and quickly examined the cut. Will tried to sound as calm and comforting as Dr. Wallace. He said, "Look here, Mr. and Mrs. Morley. This cut's not deep. It's not nearly as bad as it looks."

Mrs. Morley stopped crying and stared at Will. "It isn't?"

"No, it isn't." Will pointed at the oldest girl. "Run quick and get me some clean cloth."

She did. When she came back she handed Will a torn, laundered petticoat.

"You're brave," Will said to Amos. "You're going to stop crying now." Will ripped a large square from the petticoat and made a pad, which he pressed against the wound.

Amos looked up at Will. "Are you going to make me a big bandage?" he asked.

"A great big bandage. Everyone will see it," Will said, and smiled.

Amos looked pleased. "I went out to the privy," he said. "Somebody left the ax lying in the way. I tripped and fell on it."

Didn't the Morleys ever clean up their property or put anything away? Will wondered. Then he remembered Dr. Wallace's words. *Mend, don't pry.*

Mr. Morley looked embarrassed. "All of you hush, now," he ordered the other sniffling children. "You heard Will. Amos is going to be all right."

Dr. Wallace soon arrived and set to work. In a

short time, with Will's help, Amos's wound was stitched and bandaged.

Will edged toward the door. He knew there was a small chance that the circus wagons hadn't left yet. Maybe he could run and catch up with them. Maybe . . . But he stayed where he was until Dr. Wallace was ready to leave.

Eugene's face was red with embarrassment as he sidled up to Will. In a voice so low that no one but Will could hear him, Eugene said, "Don't blame my pa for what happened to Amos. It was my fault. I was supposed to put the ax away."

"You didn't have to tell me," Will said. "Accidents happen."

Eugene shot a quick look in his father's direction, and Will could see a flash of fear. Mr. Morley was probably going to punish Eugene. Maybe that was why Eugene was a bully—because his father was a bully too.

"Thanks for helping Amos," Eugene mumbled.

Dr. Wallace put an arm around Will's shoulders as they left the house. "I'm proud of you, son," he said.

Will pulled away and looked into Dr. Wallace's eyes. "You didn't ask me what I was doing on the road," he said.

"I didn't have to," Dr. Wallace said. "I'm pretty sure you were going to join your father. Isn't that right?"

Will gasped in surprise. "You knew about my father?"

"Miss Kelly told us he was a trick rider with a circus. The notices with the name Jesse Scott on them told us the rest."

"You didn't try to stop me," Will said.

"You're not our prisoner, Will," Dr. Wallace said slowly. "If you want to go with your real father, then Sara and I won't stand in your way."

Will gulped. His throat hurt and it was hard to swallow. "You wouldn't miss me?"

"I didn't say that," Dr. Wallace answered. Again he put an arm around Will's shoulders. This time Will didn't shrug it away.

"There would have been many tears," Dr. Wallace said. "There already have been many tears. Sara is taking your decision very hard."

Dr. Wallace paused as they reached his buggy. "You were unable to do what you wanted because you stopped to help save a life. Now, if you wish, Snow and I will take you to your father. We'll follow the tent show until we catch up. You can meet him as you had planned."

"I'd like to go to him," Will said.

Dr. Wallace nodded and led the way to the buggy.

Neither of them spoke, but as they neared the site of the tent show, Will leaned forward eagerly. There were lights! And people milling around! The wagons hadn't left!

As Dr. Wallace guided Snow onto the grounds, Jesse ran toward them.

"Willie!" he shouted. "I thought you weren't coming."

"Dr. Wallace," Will said, "this is my father, Jesse Scott."

Jesse took a step backward. He eyed Dr. Wallace uneasily. "If you've come for payment, I haven't got it," he said. "Cash is short, and I—"

"I don't want your money," Dr. Wallace said.

"Having Will as part of our family was our reward. I brought him to you, because that is what he wants. My wife and I love him. We'll miss him greatly."

Surprised, Will put a hand on Dr. Wallace's arm. "I'm not going to leave," he said. "I just wanted to say good-bye to Jesse."

Will jumped from the buggy to face Jesse. "I'm glad that you want me to go with you," he said. "I love you, Jesse. But I want to stay here."

"All right, Will," Jesse said. "I understand. It's for the best."

From the darkness someone yelled, "Hurry up, Jesse!"

Jesse shrugged. "You'll be missing out on some fun, Willie boy," he said. He broke into a teasing smile. "On the other hand, it might have been hard to find a job you could do well enough to earn your keep."

"Jesse!" the voice yelled again. "Come on! You're holding us up!"

"Good-bye, Jesse," Will said. He reached out to hug his father.

"Good-bye, Willie," Jessie said. He ruffled Will's hair, pulled away, and ran toward the wagons.

Will climbed back into the buggy. He said to Dr. Wallace, "I love Jesse, and I always will. But I want to stay with *you*, Father."

Dr. Wallace cleared his throat, and he blinked hard. "You called me *Father*," he said.

Will smiled up at him. "You're the only one who's ever called me *son.*"

EPILOGUE

Dear Miss Kelly,

Do you remember when I told you that someday my father would come for me? Carnaby's Traveling Tent Show did come to town, just like I knew it would. And Jesse said he'd ask Mr. Carnaby to give me a job, and I could come with him.

It may seem strange to you, after all that I said to you about going away with Jesse, but I changed my mind. I decided to stay with Dr. and Mrs. Wallace.

I love Jesse, and he'll always be my father. But Dr. Wallace is my father, too. I want to be a doctor like him. I want to be a good, kind man exactly like him. I'll still be at the Wallaces' if you want to write back.

Hoping that everything is well with you,
Your friend,

Will Scott

Glossary

calliope *ka-li'-o-pe* A set of steam-driven whistles activated by a keyboard.

challenge *chal'-enj* A call to win, to achieve success.

clapper *klap'-er* The tongue of a bell.

congestion *kon-jes'-tion* A disease of the lungs.

entertainer *en-ter-ta'-ner* A person who performs for others.

equinox *e'-qwa-noks* The times of equal days and nights. The vernal equinox is in March, the autumnal equinox in September.

inkwell *ingk-wel* A container for ink in which to dip a pen before writing.

kerosene *ker'-o-sen* A liquid used as a fuel in lamps.

liniment *lin´-i-ment* Liquid medication to be rubbed on the skin.

mechanic *me-kan´-ik* A device used in training circus riders.

performance *per-for´-mans* A dramatic, musical, or other entertainment.

poultice *pol´-tis* A soft, wet mixture of flour, herbs, or other ingredients, wrapped in a cloth and laid on skin to draw infection from the body.

responsible *re-spon´-si-bul* Reliable or dependable.

ringmaster *ring´-mas-ter* The person who is in charge of a circus performance.

scythe *sīth* A long, curved blade fastened to a handle; used for cutting grain or grass.

tourniquet *tur´-na-ket* a bandage, tightened by twisting, that stops the flow of blood.

The Story of
the Orphan Trains

In 1850 there were five hundred thousand people living in New York City. Ten thousand of these people were homeless children.

Many of these children were immigrants—they had come to the United States with their families from other countries. Many lived in one-room apartments. These rooms had stoves for heating and cooking, but the only water was in troughs in the hallways. These apartments were called tenements, and they were often crowded together in neighborhoods.

Immigrant parents worked long hours for very low wages. Sometimes they had barely enough money to buy food. Everyone in the family over the age of ten was expected to work. Few of these children could attend school, and many could not read or write.

Girls took in bundles of cloth from clothing

A New York City "street arab."
Courtesy the Children's Aid Society

City. Many street arabs, as they were called, turned to lives of crime.

Charles Loring Brace, a young minister and social worker, became aware of this situation. He worried about these children, who so badly needed care. With the help of some friends he founded the Children's Aid Society. The Children's Aid Society provided a place to live for some of the homeless children. It also set up industrial schools to train the children of the very poor in job skills.

Charles Loring Brace soon realized, however, that these steps were not enough. He came up with the idea of giving homeless, orphaned children a second—and much better—chance at life by taking them out of the city and placing them in homes in rural areas of the country.

Brace hired a scout to visit some of the farm communities west of New York State. He asked the scout to find out if people would be interested in taking orphan children into their homes. The scout was surprised by how many people wanted the children.

One woman wrote, "Last year was a very hard

Charles Loring Brace, founder of the Children's Aid Society
and the orphan train program.
Courtesy the Children's Aid Society

A boy proudly holds up his Children's Aid Society membership card.
Courtesy the Children's Aid Society

year, and we lost many of our children. Yes, we want your children. Please send your children."

Brace went to orphans who were living on the streets and told them what he wanted to do. Children flocked to the Children's Aid Society office. "Take me," they begged. "Please take me."

"Where do you live?" the children were asked.

The answer was always the same: "Don't live nowhere."

The first orphan train was sent west in 1856, and the last one in 1929. During these years more than a hundred and fifty thousand children were taken out of New York City by the Children's Aid Society. Another hundred thousand children were sent by train to new homes in the West by the New York Foundling Home. By 1929, states had established welfare laws and had begun taking care of people in need, so the orphan trains were discontinued.

Before a group of children was sent west by train, notices that the children were coming would be placed in the newspapers of towns along the route: "WANTED: HOMES FOR CHILDREN," one notice said. It then listed the Society's rules. Children were to be treated as members of the family. They were to be taken to church on Sundays and sent to school until they were fourteen.

Handbills were posted in the towns where the orphan train stopped, where people could easily see

Boys on board an orphan train.
Courtesy the Children's Aid Society

them. One said: "CHILDREN WITHOUT HOMES. A number of the Children brought from New York are still without homes. Friends from the country, please call and see them."

A committee of local citizens would be chosen at each of the towns. The members of the committee

Families that wanted to adopt an orphan train rider
had to follow rules such as these.
Courtesy the Children's Aid Society

were given the responsibility of making sure that the people who took the orphan train children in were good people.

Most committee members tried to do a good job. But sometimes a child was placed in a home that turned out to be unhappy. Some farmers wanted free labor and were unkind to the boys they chose. But there were many good people who wanted to provide loving homes for the orphans.

Many people were so happy with their children that they took a step beyond being foster parents and legally adopted them.

Not all the children who were taken west on the orphan trains were orphans. Some had one or both parents still living. But sometimes fathers and mothers brought their children to the Children's Aid Society.

"I can't take care of my children," they would say. "I want them to have a much better life than I can give them. Please take them west to a new home."

What did the orphan train children think about their new lives? What made the biggest impression on them? They were used to living in small spaces, surrounded by many people in a noisy, crowded city. Were they overwhelmed by the sight of miles of open countryside?

Many of them had never tasted an apple. How did they react when they saw red apples growing on trees?

When they sat down to a meal with their new

A group of children ready to board the orphan trains,
and their placing-out agents.
Courtesy the Children's Aid Society

families, did they stuff themselves? And did they feel a little guilty, remembering the small portions of food their parents had to eat?

Were they afraid to approach the large farm animals? What was it like for them to milk a cow for the first time?

WHAT IS NEEDED

Money is needed to carry forward this great child-saving enterprise. With more confidence do we ask it, since it has been so clearly shown that this work of philanthropy is not a dead weight upon the community. Though its chief aim is to rescue the helpless child victims of our social errors, it also makes a distinct economic return in the reduction of the number of those who are hopeless charges upon the common purse. More money at our command means more power to extend this great opportunity of help to the many homeless children in the boys' and girls' lodging houses in New York, and in the asylums and institutions throughout the State. We therefore ask the public for a more liberal support of this noble charity, confident that every dollar invested will bring a double return in the best kind of help to the children, so pitifully in need of it.

TABLE SHOWING THE NUMBER OF CHILDREN AND POOR FAMILIES SENT TO EACH STATE

New York	33,053	North Dakota	975
New Jersey	4,977	South Dakota	43
Pennsylvania	2,679	Kentucky	212
Maryland	563	Georgia	317
Delaware	833	Tennessee	233
District of Columbia	172	Mississippi	210
Canada	566	Florida	600
Maine	43	Alabama	50
New Hampshire	136	North Carolina	144
Vermont	262	South Carolina	191
Rhode Island	340	Louisiana	70
Massachusetts	375	Indian Territory	59
Connecticut	1,588	Oklahoma	95
Ohio	7,272	Arkansas	136
Indiana	3,955	Montana	83
Illinois	9,172	Wyoming	19
Iowa	6,675	Colorado	1,563
Missouri	6,088	Utah	31
Nebraska	3,442	Idaho	52
Minnesota	3,258	Washington	231
Kansas	4,150	Nevada	59
Michigan	5,326	Oregon	90
Wisconsin	2,750	California	168
Virginia	1,634	New Mexico	1
West Virginia	149	Texas	1,527

This chart, from the Children's Aid Society's 1910 bulletin, shows the number of children who rode the orphan trains and the states to which they were sent.

Courtesy the Children's Aid Society

Three sisters who were taken in by the
Children's Aid Society after their
mother had died. At the time the
photograph was taken, the two youngest
girls had been adopted.
Courtesy the Children's Aid Society

During the first few years of the orphan trains,
the records kept by the Children's Aid Society were
not complete. In a later survey taken in 1917, the
Children's Aid Society researched what had happened to many of the orphan train children who
had grown up.

He found that among them were a governor of North Dakota, a governor of the Territory of Alaska, two members of the United States Congress, nine members of state legislatures, two district attorneys, two mayors, a justice of the Supreme Court, four judges, many college professors, teachers, journalists, bankers, doctors, attorneys, four army officers, and seven thousand soldiers and sailors.

Although there were some problems in this system of matching homeless children with foster parents, the orphan train program did what it set out to do. It gave the homeless children of New York City the chance to live much better lives.

The younger children placed out by the Society always show a very large average of success. The great proportion have grown up respectable men and women, creditable members of society. Many of them have been legally adopted by their foster parents. The majority have become successful farmers or farmers' wives, mechanics and business men. Many have acquired property, and no inconsiderable number of them have attained positions of honor and trust.

NOTEWORTHY CAREERS

Governor of a State 1	Bankers 29
Governor of a Territory 1	Physicians 19
Members of Congress 2	Lawyers 35
Judges 4	Sheriffs 2
Justice of Supreme Court 1	Postmasters 9
Members of State Legislatures . . . 9	Army Officers 9
	Government Transportation Clerk . .
Auditor General (State) 1	 1
Mayor 1	Railroad Officials 6
Clerk of Senate 1	Railroad Men 36
County Treasurer 1	Real Estate Agents 10
County Auditors 3	Journalists 16
County Recorder 1	Teachers 86
County Superintendent of Education	
. . . . 1	High School Principals 7
County Clerk 1	Superintendents of Schools 2
County Commissioners 3	College Professors 2
City Attorney 1	Civil Engineers 3
District Attorneys 2	Clergymen 24
Business Clerks 465	Merchants 23

About 3,500 entered the Army and Navy.

This chart from the Children's Aid Society's 1910 bulletin shows the careers of some of the orphan train riders. (Note: This survey was taken seven years earlier than the survey mentioned on pages 112-113.)
Courtesy the Children's Aid Society

American Schools in the 1860s

Young people in the United States today are required to go to school for at least ten years. But in the 1860s, things were different. Most children started school at age six or seven and continued until age fourteen. Laws that required children to attend school weren't adopted throughout the country until the early twentieth century.

In New York City, a boy like Will would probably have gone to a public school. Public schools (schools funded by the state) began to be established in the United States in the early 1800s. But not all New York City children could go to school in 1866. At that time, schools in the city were flooded with immigrant children—there wasn't enough room for everyone who wanted to go. To educate as many as possible, some schools held two half-day sessions instead of one full day.

Students who didn't live in big cities usually were either taught at home by their parents or attended school in a one- or two-room building (like

EX-GOVERNOR JOHN G. BRADY.

12— John Brady, half-orphan, was deserted by his father at the age of 10 years. He was placed with Mr. John Green, of Tipton, Indiana. Remained on the farm until 1867, and then taught school. In 1870 went to Yale College, graduating in 1874, when he entered Union Seminary. After he was ordained he went as a missionary to Alaska. 1897 he was appointed Governor of Alaska by President McKinley. Reappointed by President Roosevelt, serving three terms.

25

John G. Brady was an orphan train rider who became governor of Alaska.
Courtesy the Children's Aid Society

the school Will goes to in Barkerville, Missouri). Children at schools like Will's were often needed at home to work on the family farm, so their school year was usually shorter than that of city students.

The oral exam that Mr. Schultz gives to Will to find out what grade he should be in was common practice. The first printed school exams were used in Boston in 1845, but most exams were given orally.

Rural schools had very strong ties to the communities they operated in. Parents would help build the schoolhouse and even help choose the teacher. The teachers often took turns living with families in the community. Mrs. Schultz tells Will that she can't wait until school begins again because of the "box suppers and talent shows and spelling bees." In the 1860s, there was no television or radio, so a school like Will's was often the entertainment center of the community.

Going west on the orphan train could be a real improvement in the life of an orphan who couldn't attend school in the city he or she came from. Many orphans lived on the streets before they went

EX-GOVERNOR ANDREW H. BURKE.

13— Andrew H. Burke, when at the age of 10½, an orphan, was placed with Mr. D. W. Butler, then transferred to Mr. E. K. Hall, of Noblesville, Indiana.

1863—Went into the army as a drummer boy.

1868—Attending college at Greencastle, Indiana.

1881—Cashier of bank for 3 years.

1884—Elected County Treasurer, which position he held continuously for 6 years.

November, 1890—Elected Governor of North Dakota.

26

Andrew H. Burke was an orphan train rider who became
governor of North Dakota.
Courtesy the Children's Aid Society

west. They had too many worries just trying to survive, much less attend school. Other orphan train riders couldn't get a decent education because the city schools were so crowded. Many of the children who went west thrived in their new atmosphere. Able to attend smaller schools and receive individual attention from their teachers, many of the orphan train riders achieved great success as adults.

SOURCES:

Education in Rural America: A Reassessment of Conventional Wisdom, edited by Jonathan P. Sher, Boulder, Colorado: Westview Press, 1977.

The Encyclopedia Americana, International Edition, Danbury, Connecticut: Grolier Incorporated, 1996.

The Encyclopedia of New York City, edited by Kenneth T. Jackson, New Haven & London: Yale University Press; New York: The New York Historical Society, 1995.

The Children's Aid Society is still active today, helping more than 100,000 New York City children and their families each year. The Society's services include adoption and foster care, medical and dental care, counseling, preventive services, winter and summer camps, recreation, cultural enrichment, education, and job training.

For more information, contact:

The Children's Aid Society
105 East 22nd Street
New York, NY 10010
